I0663299

The Festival

*A Lovecraftian Horror Story of Ancient
Rituals and Dark Secrets*

A Modern Translation

Adapted for the Contemporary Reader

H.P. Lovecraft

Translated by Tim Zengerink

Table of Contents

Preface - Message to the Reader

What If You Could Help Rebuild the Greatest Library in Human History?

Thousands of years ago, the Library of Alexandria stood as the crown jewel of human achievement — a sanctuary where the collected wisdom of every known civilization was gathered, preserved, and shared freely.

And then, it was lost.

Through fire, conquest, and the slow erosion of time, humanity lost not just books — but ideas, dreams, discoveries, and stories that could have changed the world forever.

Today, the Library of Alexandria lives again — and you are invited to be a part of its restoration.

Our mission is simple yet profound:

To rebuild the greatest library the world has ever known, and to translate all timeless works into every language and dialect, so that no seeker of knowledge is ever left behind again.

By joining our movement to rebuild the modern Library of Alexandria, you become part of an unprecedented mission:

- **Unlimited Access to the Greatest Audiobooks & eBooks Ever Written:**

  Instantly explore thousands of legendary works—Plato, Shakespeare, Jane Austen, Leo Tolstoy, and countless more. All instantly available to read or listen, placing a complete literary universe at your fingertips.

- **Beautiful Paperback & Deluxe Editions at Printing Cost**

  Own any title as an elegant paperback, deluxe hardcover, or stunning collectible boxset—offered to you at true printing cost, delivered straight to your door. Build your personal Library of Alexandria, crafted for beauty, built for durability, and worthy of proud display.

- **Fresh Translations for Modern Readers—in Every Language & Dialect**

  Enjoy timeless masterpieces reimagined in clear, contemporary language—no more outdated phrases or obscure references. Alongside the original versions, we're tirelessly translating these classics into every language and dialect imaginable, ensuring accessibility and understanding across cultures and generations.

- **Join a Global Renaissance of Literature & Knowledge**

  You directly support expanding our library, publishing deluxe editions at true cost, translating works into all global languages, and bringing humanity's greatest stories to people everywhere. By joining today, you're not just preserving a legacy of masterpieces; you set in motion a powerful wave of literary accessibility.

Become a Torchbearer of Knowledge.

Join us for free now at **LibraryofAlexandria.com**

Together, we will ensure that the light of human wisdom never fades again.

With gratitude and a shared love of knowledge,

The Modern Library of Alexandria Team

Visit:

www.libraryofalexandria.com

Or scan the code below:

Introduction

The Oldest Fear: Ritual, Ancestry, and the Return of the Hidden Gods

H.P. Lovecraft's "The Festival," first published in the January 1925 issue of Weird Tales, is one of the earliest fully realized expressions of what would become Lovecraft's distinctive brand of cosmic horror. In this short but haunting tale, we find the foundational elements of the mythos that would define his later work: ancient rites performed in decaying towns, traditions predating human memory, and terrifying glimpses into realities beyond human comprehension. While "The Festival" may not be as well-known as The Call of Cthulhu or The Shadow Over Innsmouth, it holds a crucial place in Lovecraft's literary development. It is the first of his stories to take the theme of ancestral return and ritual reenactment to its terrifying extreme.

The plot of "The Festival" is deceptively simple. A nameless narrator journeys to the coastal town of Kingsport, Massachusetts—based on Lovecraft's beloved Marblehead—during the Yule season to take part in an ancient family festival. He has been summoned by a letter from a relative he has never met, and although the town is unfamiliar, it feels disturbingly known. As he makes his way through the snow-covered streets and into the heart of the festival, he slowly discovers that the traditions he has come to observe are not merely quaint or folkloric, but remnants of a primordial order—an order that does not die, and that calls its bloodlines back to it in due time.

The horror of "The Festival" is not immediate or theatrical. It unfolds through atmosphere, implication, and slow revelation. The narrator's descent—literal and symbolic—into an underground cavern beneath the town's church becomes a metaphysical descent into the dark roots of civilization, religion, and the self. The rituals he witnesses are not of this world. The people he meets do not move like the living. And when he tries to flee, it is not freedom he finds, but madness.

This tale, like many of Lovecraft's best, is a meditation on the limits of human understanding and the terror that comes with discovering one's place in a much older and more terrifying universe. The central revelation is not a monster, but a truth: that the narrator belongs to this world, that he is not a visitor, but a participant. It is the horror of inherited guilt, ancestral debt, and bloodlines that do not die.

Kingsport and the Lovecraftian Ritual Landscape

"The Festival" is one of the first stories in which Lovecraft truly establishes the geographical and symbolic template for what would become his New England mythos. The town of Kingsport is a prototype for other locations like Innsmouth, Dunwich, and Arkham—a place where history stretches back too far, where the land itself seems to resist the present, and where the townspeople are united by secrets deeper than time. These towns are not merely settings—they are characters, haunted not only by ghosts, but by the echoes of rituals that predate all known religions.

In Kingsport, Lovecraft captures the uncanny intersection of the Puritan aesthetic and pre-human horror. The wooden houses lean unnaturally over winding cobblestone streets. The townsfolk speak in strange, archaic English. The church is not a sanctuary, but a gateway. Even the air is charged with dread. The setting is alien not because it is unfamiliar, but because it is too familiar—a version of New England that feels like it was never truly part of the modern world to begin with. In this environment, time itself becomes unreliable. History is not linear, but cyclical. Ritual is not performance, but participation in a vast and ongoing cosmic reality.

The descent beneath the church—into a crypt, a cavern, a temple—is among the most striking moments in Lovecraft's early fiction. There, the narrator encounters robed figures, indescribable architecture, and creatures that hint at the nonhuman origins of human belief. It is a scene that foreshadows the more elaborate mythological systems Lovecraft would explore in later works, particularly his ideas about the Great Old Ones, alien gods, and non-Euclidean geometry. But even here, in embryonic form, the point is clear: what humans call gods are merely ancient, indifferent forces. The rituals we inherit are not sacred—they are survival mechanisms, tenuous links to a world that should have been left forgotten.

Lovecraft was fascinated by the idea of atavism— the idea that beneath the veneer of civilization lie older instincts and older connections. In "The Festival," the narrator's journey is not simply across geography, but across time and into identity. He begins as an outsider and ends as an heir. He cannot escape what he is, and what he is, it turns out, is not fully human in the way he believed.

This is a key feature of Lovecraft's fiction: the horror is not external, but internal. The monsters are not out there, but in our history, our ancestry, our reflection. This shift from gothic horror to existential dread is what marks Lovecraft's work as truly modern—and why it continues to resonate today.

Ritual Horror, Psychological Descent, and Literary Legacy

"The Festival" is not merely a tale of strange ceremonies and monstrous revelations. It is a deeply psychological story—a study in alienation, identity, and the loss of self. The narrator, who initially views his pilgrimage to Kingsport as an act of reverence or curiosity, is slowly absorbed into a world he does not understand. By the end, his memories have been corrupted, his mind shattered, and his sense of identity dissolved. He is no longer an observer. He has become a vessel.

This trajectory—from rational witness to unknowing participant—is central to Lovecraft's philosophy of cosmic horror. Human beings, he suggests, are not the protagonists of the universe. We are not its heroes, or even its intended audience. We are incidental. The rituals we keep, the myths we preserve, and the towns we inhabit are not safeguards against the unknown. They are its disguises.

Lovecraft's style in "The Festival" is already maturing. Though still prone to purple prose and antiquarian flourishes, he exercises remarkable restraint in his descriptions. The horror is never fully named. The creatures are "things," "beings," or simply "not men." The architecture is "blasphemous," "cyclopean," or "non-Euclidean." These adjectives do not clarify—they destabilize. They invite the reader's imagination to fill in the gaps, and in doing so, they ensure that the horror remains alive and personal.

The story's closing image—the narrator fleeing into madness, unable to deny what he has seen—would become a Lovecraftian signature. The mind recoils. Sanity bends. The world does not realign. There is no comfort, only a kind of awful knowledge, and the suspicion that one day, we too might receive the call.

The influence of "The Festival" extends far beyond its relatively brief narrative. It laid the groundwork for the ritual horror subgenre, inspiring countless later works about cults, hidden rites, and ancestral hauntings. Writers like Stephen King (Jerusalem's Lot), Thomas Ligotti, Brian Lumley, Caitlín R. Kiernan, and Laird Barron have drawn directly or indirectly from

Lovecraft's ritualistic narratives. Films like The Wicker Man, The Witch, and Hereditary also trace their DNA to "The Festival," with their focus on inherited evil, secret societies, and sacrificial traditions that are terrifying precisely because they are so calmly practiced.

This modern edition presents Lovecraft's original text with carefully updated language and structure for today's reader. While preserving the voice, mood, and cadence of the original, this version smooths overly archaic constructions and clarifies ambiguous references without diluting Lovecraft's vision. The goal is not to modernize the horror, but to make its vessel more accessible—to invite a broader audience into the shadowed corridors of Kingsport and its inhuman rites.

Reading "The Festival" today is not just an exercise in literary appreciation—it is an initiation. It is a recognition that the past is not past, that some traditions are not celebratory but sacrificial, and that beneath the masks of culture lie truths far older than civilization. This story does not offer resolution. It offers revelation. And once seen, it cannot be unseen.

This edition invites you to enter Kingsport, to walk its crooked streets, and to descend, as all initiates must, into the place beneath the church. Do not expect light. Do not expect answers. Expect only the cold embrace of tradition, the whisper of the old chants, and the certainty that something waits below—something that has waited a very long time. Welcome to the Festival.

The Festival

Demons can make people see things that aren't real,
but look so real it's like they actually exist.
—Lactantius.

I was far from home, and I couldn't stop thinking about the sea. As the sky darkened, I heard the waves crashing against the rocks. I knew the ocean was just beyond the hill, where the willow trees bent in the wind under a clearing sky and the first stars began to shine. My ancestors had once called me to return to the old town beyond that hill, so I kept walking through the fresh snow on the empty road. The path climbed higher as I followed it toward the twinkling star of Aldebaran and the ancient town I had never seen, only imagined in my dreams.

It was Christmas, though deep down, people know it's older than the stories from Bethlehem or Babylon— older even than Memphis and the earliest days of people. This was the Yule season, and I had finally reached the old town by the sea where my family had once lived. A long time ago, they held celebrations there, even when it wasn't allowed. They told their children to return every hundred years so that old secrets wouldn't be forgotten. My family had been around for a long time, even before this land was settled three hundred years ago. They were different—quiet and mysterious—and had come from faraway, warm places filled with orchids. They spoke another language before learning the one spoken by the pale-eyed fishermen here. Now they were gone, and only a few still followed their old traditions. I was the only one who came back that night, just like the stories said I should.

At the top of the hill, I saw Kingsport spread out below, silent and cold in the evening light. Snow covered everything—old rooftops, tall church towers, small bridges, willow trees, and graveyards. The streets twisted and turned in all directions, filled with old houses placed like scattered blocks. At the center stood a church on a steep hill, untouched by time. The sea crashed against the aging wooden docks—the same sea that had brought my people here long ago.

Near the highest point of the road, a taller hill stood in the distance. It was bare and windswept, and I realized it was a cemetery. Black headstones stuck out of the snow like decaying fingernails from a giant buried beneath. The road was quiet and empty, and now and then, I thought I heard a strange creaking sound, like a rope swinging in the wind. I remembered that four of my relatives had been hanged for witchcraft in 1692, though I didn't know exactly where it had happened.

As I headed down the slope toward the sea, I listened for the sounds of people talking or laughing, but the village was still. Then I thought about the time of year and figured these old-fashioned people probably spent Christmas in quiet prayer around their fireplaces. So I stopped hoping for music or voices, and just kept walking past still farmhouses and dark stone fences. I made my way to the older part of town, where signs above the shops creaked in the breeze, and strange door knockers gleamed under the soft light of windows hidden behind curtains.

I had looked at maps before, so I knew how to find my family's old house. I'd been told they would know me and welcome me, since stories last a long time in small towns. I walked quickly through Back Street to Circle Court, then across the only full stone sidewalk in town, heading to Green Lane behind the Market House. I was glad I had walked. The village had looked beautiful from the hill, and now I was eager to reach the seventh house on the left—the one with the steep roof and upper floor that stuck out over the street. It had been built before 1650.

When I got there, I saw lights shining through the windows. The diamond-shaped glass showed that the house still looked the same after all these years. The second floor reached out over the narrow road and almost touched the house across from it, making the space feel like a tunnel. The stone step was clear of snow. There were no sidewalks, but some houses had high doors with two sets of stairs and iron railings. The place looked strange to me—I'd never seen anything quite like it in New England. Even though I liked how it looked, I would have felt more comfortable if there had been footprints in the snow, people outside, or windows left open without curtains.

***

When I knocked on the old iron door knocker, I felt nervous. Something about the quiet, the cold evening, and the strange traditions of the town had built up a sense of fear inside me. And when the door creaked open without any sound of footsteps beforehand, that fear grew stronger. But it didn't last long. An old man stood in the doorway, wearing a robe and soft slippers. His calm, quiet expression helped me feel a little more at ease. He didn't speak, but instead used a wax tablet and a pointed tool to write a polite, old-fashioned welcome. I realized then that he couldn't talk.

He motioned for me to come inside, into a low-ceilinged room lit by candles. Thick wooden beams crossed the ceiling, and the furniture looked stiff and dark, like it hadn't been touched since the 1600s. Everything felt like a piece of the past—nothing was missing. There was a huge fireplace, and near it sat a hunched old woman wearing a loose robe and a deep bonnet, slowly spinning thread on a wheel. She didn't speak or look up, even though it was the holiday season. The room felt cold and damp, and I was surprised there wasn't a fire going. A tall wooden bench faced a row of curtained windows on the left side, and it seemed like someone might be sitting there, though I couldn't be sure. I didn't like the feeling in that room. The fear I thought I'd gotten past began creeping back in.

Strangely, it was the old man's calm face that made me feel even more unsettled. The longer I looked at him, the less human he seemed. His eyes didn't move at all, and his skin looked too smooth—almost like wax. Eventually, I became convinced that it wasn't a real face, but a carefully made mask. Still, his soft, gloved hands kept writing friendly notes on the tablet, saying I needed to wait before I'd be taken to the celebration.

He pointed to a chair and a table with a pile of books, then left the room. I sat down and started to read, but the books were dusty, old, and covered in mold. I saw titles I'd only heard of in whispers—Marvels of Science by Morryster, Saducismus Triumphatus by Joseph Glanvil from 1681, Daemonolatreia by Remigius printed in 1595, and worst of all, the infamous Necronomicon by the mad Arab Abdul Alhazred, translated into Latin by Olaus Wormius. I had never seen that book before, but I'd heard frightening things about it.

No one spoke to me. I only heard the wind shaking the signs outside and the soft whir of the spinning wheel as the old woman kept working without a word. The room, the books, and the people all felt gloomy and strange, but I reminded myself that this gathering had been called by an old family tradition, and I should be ready for unusual things. So I tried to read. But when I found something terrifying in the Necronomicon— something so awful it didn't even feel real—it shook me deeply. I thought I heard one of the windows slowly close, like someone had opened it quietly and was now trying not to be noticed. This happened right after a strange spinning noise, one that didn't come from the woman's wheel. It wasn't much, though—the old woman was spinning quickly, and the old clock had been chiming.

After that, I stopped feeling like there was anyone on the bench near the windows. I was still reading,

18

shivering from what I had found, when the old man returned. He was now wearing boots and a loose old-fashioned outfit, and he sat on the bench, blocking him from my view. Waiting in that room felt tense, and having that cursed book in my hands only made it worse.

When the clock struck eleven, the old man stood up, went to a large carved chest in the corner, and pulled out two cloaks with hoods. He put one on himself and gently wrapped the other around the old woman, who was finally stopping her endless spinning. She walked slowly and stiffly, while the old man, now with his hood over his still, lifeless face—or mask—picked up the Necronomicon and motioned for me to follow.

We stepped out into the dark, winding streets of the ancient town, just as the lights in the curtained windows were going out one by one. The Dog Star shone brightly above us as silent figures wearing cloaks and hoods began pouring out of every doorway. They moved in eerie processions down narrow streets and past creaky signs, old rooftops, and tiny windows with diamond-shaped glass. They traveled through steep alleys where crumbling houses leaned on each other, and across open courtyards and graveyards where lanterns bobbed, casting strange lights like twisted constellations.

I followed my silent guides through the crowd. The people brushed against me—soft arms, oddly mushy bodies—but I never saw a single face or heard a voice. The strange lines of people moved upward, twisting and turning, all heading toward one spot at the top of the highest hill in town. There, perched above it all, stood a large white church. I had seen it earlier from the road and had shivered then, too, because it looked like the star Aldebaran had paused for a moment right on its pale spire.

There was an open area around the church—part graveyard with ghostly tombstones, part uneven square where the wind had swept away most of the snow. Along the edges stood old, creepy houses with sharp rooftops and heavy overhangs. Strange lights flickered above the graves, showing disturbing views of the cemetery, but oddly, they didn't create any shadows. Beyond the graveyard, where there were no buildings, I could look out past the hilltop and see stars shining faintly over the harbor, even though the town itself was hidden in the darkness. Now and then, a single lantern would float eerily through winding paths, heading to catch up with the silent crowd that was already slipping into the church.

I waited until everyone had gone inside—even the stragglers at the back. The old man tugged at my sleeve, but I wanted to be the last to enter. Finally, I stepped forward, following the strange man and the old woman who had been spinning yarn. As I crossed the doorway into that packed, shadowy church, I glanced back one last time. The faint glow from the graveyard cast a pale light on the path behind me. I shivered. Though most of the snow had been blown away, a few patches still clung to the ground near the entrance. In that quick glance, it struck me that there were no footprints—not even my own.

Inside, the lanterns barely lit the space. Most of the crowd had already disappeared. They had moved quickly up the main aisle between tall white pews, heading straight for a trapdoor in the floor just in front of the pulpit. It was wide open, leading down into the dark below, and the people were silently slipping through. I followed without thinking, stepping down worn stone stairs into a cold, stale underground chamber. The back end of the moving crowd looked disturbingly unnatural, and watching them slide into an old tomb made my skin crawl. Then I saw that the floor of the tomb had an opening, and everyone was quietly going down a steep staircase carved from rough stone.

We descended deeper and deeper. The narrow stairs twisted tightly in a spiral, and the air grew damp and foul. The stone walls dripped with moisture, and the mortar between the blocks looked like it had started to crumble. After what felt like forever, I realized the walls and steps had changed—they were now carved directly from solid rock. What disturbed me most was the silence. The steps of all those people made no sound. Nothing echoed. It was like the place swallowed all noise.

Eventually, narrow side tunnels started to appear, branching off from the staircase. They looked like secret passages leading into complete darkness. There were more and more of them, and they reminded me of ancient underground graveyards filled with unknown threats. The air smelled so strongly of rot that it made me gag. I was certain we had passed beneath the hill, under the entire town of Kingsport, and the thought of that old place hiding such a decaying underworld sent chills through me.

Then I saw a strange, flickering light ahead and heard the faint sound of water gently splashing. I shivered again. I hated everything this night had shown me and wished more than anything that my ancestors had never called me to be part of this eerie ritual. As the tunnel widened and the stairs leveled out, I heard a new sound—a weak, high-pitched flute playing a tune that didn't sound human. And then, all at once, the path opened into a huge underground world. I stood at the edge of a strange shore, covered in fungi and lit by a thick green flame rising from the ground. Before me stretched a dark, oily river, flowing from deep, hidden places and heading into the blackest parts of an ancient, forgotten sea.

***

Weak and barely able to breathe, I stared at the strange underground world full of giant mushrooms, sickly green flames, and dark, slimy water. Around the glowing fire, I saw crowds in hooded cloaks standing in a half-circle. They were performing the Yule ritual—something older than humanity, meant to outlast it. It was a celebration tied to the winter solstice and the coming of spring, a tradition of fire, greenery, light, and music. In that dark cave, I watched them carry out the rite. They bowed before the strange flame, tossing handfuls of thick, glowing plants into the water. Far from the fire, I noticed something shapeless sitting in the shadows, playing a shrill tune on a flute. As it played, I thought I heard strange wings flapping in the dark, though I couldn't see anything.

What scared me most wasn't the creature or the crowd—but the flame itself. It shot up like a volcano from some deep, unknown place, yet gave off no heat or light that felt alive. It didn't make shadows, and instead of warmth, it spread a cold dampness, like the chill of death. The rocks above it were stained green with something that looked poisonous.

The old man who had brought me slithered to the front, right beside the flame. He raised his arms in stiff, practiced movements toward the crowd. At key points in the ceremony, the others bowed low to the ground, especially when he lifted the Necronomicon, the awful book he had brought. I joined in the bowing too, since my ancestors had called me here through their writings. Then the old man gave a signal to the flute-player in the shadows, who changed the tune slightly—just enough to trigger something horrible and unexpected. The moment it happened, I nearly collapsed onto the mossy ground, overwhelmed by a fear that didn't belong to this world, but to the empty spaces between the stars.

From the endless black beyond the sick glow of that cold fire, from the cursed lands where the oily river flowed unseen and unknown, came a swarm of strange, flapping creatures. They moved in a rhythm, as if trained. Their shapes were impossible to fully understand—part bird, part bat, part insect, maybe even part human, but none of those exactly. They crawled and flew awkwardly, using both webbed feet and leathery wings. As they reached the group, the hooded people climbed onto their backs and rode them away, disappearing one by one along the dark river. They vanished into tunnels and caves filled with panic and poison, into places no map could ever show.

The old woman had already left with the others, and the only reason the old man remained was because I had refused to ride one of those creatures. When I finally stood, I saw that the flute-player had vanished too, but two of the animals still waited nearby. As I held back, the old man took out his tablet and wrote that he was the chosen one of my ancestors, the same ones who had started this Yule ritual long ago. He told me I had been meant to return, and that the deepest secrets were still to come. His handwriting was old and formal. When I didn't move, he reached into his robe and pulled out a seal ring and a pocket watch, both marked with my family crest. But the sight of them terrified me—because I knew that watch had been buried with my great-great-great-great-grandfather back in 1698.

Then he pulled back his hood and pointed to his face, trying to show me how he looked like our family. But I didn't believe it. That face was too smooth, too fake. I was sure it was just a wax mask hiding something worse. The creatures were growing restless, scratching at the moss-covered ground, and the old man was getting just as twitchy. When one of the beasts started to wander off, he moved quickly to stop it, and the sudden motion knocked the mask off his head.

What I saw underneath froze me in place—and blocked the only path back to the stairs. With no other choice, I threw myself into the black, greasy river that twisted its way through the underground caves. I plunged into that filthy stream full of ancient terrors, hoping to escape whatever nightmare was about to come for me, before my screams brought the attention of whatever other horrors hid in those cursed tunnels.

***

At the hospital, they told me they found me at dawn, nearly frozen, holding onto a piece of floating wood in Kingsport Harbor. They believed I had taken the wrong turn on a hill road the night before and fallen off the cliffs at Orange Point. They said the footprints in the snow led them to that conclusion. I couldn't argue, but everything felt wrong. From the large window, I could see rooftops, but only a few looked like the old houses I remembered. I heard the hum of cars and the clang of trolleys down below. They kept saying this was Kingsport, and even though I didn't believe it, I had no way to prove otherwise.

When I started panicking after they told me the hospital was near the old cemetery on Central Hill, they transferred me to St. Mary's Hospital in Arkham. They thought I'd get better care there. I actually liked it. The doctors were understanding and even helped me borrow a rare copy of Alhazred's disturbing Necronomicon from the Miskatonic University library. They believed I was dealing with some sort of mental illness and thought reading the book again might help me process it.

So I read the same terrifying chapter—and it disturbed me more than ever, because I realized it wasn't new to me. I had seen it before, no matter what the snowy footprints said. Where I saw it is something I wish I could forget. No one around me could ever remind me of that place—but in my sleep, I still see it. My dreams are filled with fear, filled with phrases I refuse to repeat. There's only one part I'm willing to translate, in the clearest English I can manage from the strange, broken Latin:

"The deepest parts of the earth are not meant to be seen by human eyes. What's down there is strange and terrifying. The ground is cursed where dead thoughts come back in twisted shapes. And cursed is a mind that exists without a body. Ibn Schacabac once said that the safest grave is one untouched by magic, and the safest town at night is one where no wizards remain. Old stories say that when someone sells their soul, the spirit doesn't leave the body right away. It stays behind, feeding the worms that eat it—teaching them, changing them. From the rot, something evil grows. These things become smarter and more dangerous, growing bigger and more twisted. Secret tunnels are dug where the ground should have been solid, and now things that were meant to crawl have learned how to walk."

Thank You for Reading

Dear Reader,

We hope this timeless classic has sparked your imagination and enriched your literary journey. Now that you've turned the final page, we want to share a vision for the future of reading—one where every classic you've ever wanted to explore is at your fingertips, in a format that best suits your life.

We'd like to invite you to gain immediate, unlimited digital & audiobook access to hundreds of the most treasured literary classics ever written—along with the option to secure deluxe paperback, hardcover & box set editions at printing cost. Together, we can spark a new global literary renaissance alongside our small, independent publishing house called "The Library of Alexandria."

Thousands of years ago, the Library of Alexandria stood as a beacon of knowledge—until it was lost to history. We aim to reignite that spirit of preservation and discovery right now, in the modern age—only this time, it's accessible to all, in every language and every format.

Picture a world where every timeless classic, novel, poem, or philosophical treatise is not only available to read but also updated for today's readers—modernized, translated into any language or dialect, and ready to enjoy in any format you choose, whether that is in an eBook, audiobook, paperback, or deluxe hardcover & box set version a printing cost.

By joining our movement to rebuild the modern Library of Alexandria, you become part of an unprecedented mission to offer:

- **Unlimited Audiobook & eBook Access to the Greatest Classics of All Time**

  Instantly explore thousands of legendary works, from Plato and Shakespeare to Jane Austen and Leo Tolstoy. All are instantly ready to read or listen to, giving you a complete literary universe at your fingertips.

- **Paperback & Deluxe Editions at Printing Costs:**

  Purchase any title in a paperback, deluxe hardbound, or deluxe boxset edition at printing costs, shipped right to your doorstep. Curate your personal library of Alexandria with editions worthy of display—crafted to last, designed to captivate, and delivered straight to your door.

- **Modern translations for Contemporary Readers in all languages and dialects**

  Discover a vast selection of classics reimagined in clear, current language—no more struggling with outdated phrases or obscure references. Next to the original versions, we aim to offer translations in as many languages and dialects as possible.

  As we continue our translation efforts and add new languages, readers everywhere can connect with these works as if they were written today. By bridging linguistic divides, you're contributing to ensuring that these timeless stories become more meaningful, accessible, and inspiring for people across the globe.

- **Your Personal Library of Alexandria:**

  Over the months and years, you'll curate a unique physical archive of classics—each volume a testament to your taste, curiosity, and love of knowledge. It's not just about owning books—it's about curating a cultural legacy you'll cherish and pass down for generations to come.

- **Join a Global Literary Renaissance:**

  Your support fuels an ongoing mission: allowing us to reinvest in offering deluxe print editions (including special boxsets) at their true cost, broaden the range of available formats and translations, and extend the reach of these works to new audiences worldwide. By joining today, you're not just preserving a legacy of masterpieces; you set in motion a powerful wave of literary accessibility.

We are more than a publisher—we're a movement, and we can't do it alone. Your support lets us scale our mission, preserving and reimagining history's greatest works for tomorrow's readers.

Become a Torchbearer of knowledge.

Thank you for picking up this book and allowing us into your literary journey. As you turn the pages, know that you're part of something larger: a global effort to keep these stories alive, share their wisdom across borders and generations, and spark a true cultural revival for the modern era.

If this resonates with you—please consider taking the next step by visiting:

www.libraryofalexandria.com

With gratitude and a shared love of knowledge,

The Modern Library of Alexandria Team

Visit:

www.libraryofalexandria.com

Or scan the code below: